HORRIBLE HARRY AND THE GREEN SLIME

BY SUZY KLINE

Pictures by Frank Remkiewicz

Puffin Books

PUFFIN BOOKS
Published by the Penguin Group
Penguin Putnam Inc., 375 Hudson Street, New York, New York 10014, U.S.A.
Penguin Books Ltd, 27 Wrights Lane, London W8 5TZ, England
Penguin Books Australia Ltd, Ringwood, Victoria, Australia
Penguin Books Canada Ltd, 10 Alcorn Avenue, Toronto, Ontario, Canada M4V 3B2
Penguin Books (N.Z.) Ltd, 182-190 Wairau Road, Auckland 10, New Zealand

Penguin Books Ltd, Registered Offices: Harmondsworth, Middlesex, England

First published in the United States of America by Viking Penguin,
a division of Penguin Books USA Inc., 1989
Published in Puffin Books, 1991
Reissued 1998

3 5 7 9 10 8 6 4 2

THE LIBRARY OF CONGRESS HAS CATALOGED THE PREVIOUS PUFFIN EDITION
UNDER CATALOG CARD NUMBER: 91-52535.
This edition ISBN 0-14-038970-9

Printed in the United States of America

RL: 2.3

For my class who launched the original cobweb invasion at Southwest School,

Sarah Bene
Jeremy Brignolo
Curt Buchenholz
Erin Caruso
Desirée Celadon
Troy Clark
Danny Coury
Casey Crowly
Erin DuCotey
Kate Fasciano
Shawn Ficke
Kristin Geiger
Danielle Gerardi
Carissa Gibson
Elizabeth Hall
J.R. Herrington
Christopher Hoehne
Phillip Langin
Michelle Mahoney
Jessica Nalette
Erik Pecorelli
Tracy Richnavsky
Randy Skok
Danielle Whitney
Jared Yorkavich

Contents

Secret Pals

Miss Mackle held up a big glass jar with the names of everyone in Room 2B.

"Today," she said, "we will pick secret pals."

Everyone looked around the room and pointed at somebody.

Harry pointed at me.

I pointed at Harry.

"Just a minute," Miss Mackle continued, "when I say 'pick a pal,' I mean pick a pal out of *this* jar."

Everyone stared at the jar and groaned.

"For one week," Miss Mackle continued, "you will send letters and little homemade surprises to your secret pal. On Friday, you will bring a letter to school saying who you are. I hope this activity will promote writing skills *and* new friendships."

I put my hand in the jar very carefully. Then Harry did.

Slowly we opened the folded pieces of paper.

Harry flashed his white teeth. I could tell he was happy about the name he drew.

"I bet you have Song Lee," I whispered.

Harry nodded. "How did you guess?"

Miss Mackle put the jar back on her desk. "Now remember, boys and girls, your secret pal *is* a secret. Don't tell anyone! And when you give your pal something, make sure it is when he or she is not at their desk."

"Who do you have, Doug?" Harry whispered.

"I can't tell you. Didn't you hear the teacher?"

Harry made a face. "I told you!"

"No you didn't. I guessed yours."

"Do you have Ida?" Harry guessed.

I shook my head.

"Tell me!" Harry insisted.

"I can't."

"Then you're not my friend anymore," Harry said.

Miss Mackle stood in front of the

class. "I think this activity will be a fun learning experience."

Some fun, I thought. I just lost my best friend.

The next day when Song Lee was with her special English teacher, Harry put a fat letter on her desk with a picture of Tyrannosaurus Rex.

Harry found a letter on his desk. He read it aloud:

Dear Harry,

You make good snoballs
You rite good storys about
the sea You make Room 2B
fun

Your Secret Pal

?

Here is a
seashell for you
It is a Conch.

Harry leaned over on his desk, "See Doug, *my* pal knows how to be a friend. He's not like YOU!"

And then he picked up the conch and listened to the sounds of the sea.

He didn't even ask me if I wanted a turn.

When I came back from lunch, I found a drawing on my desk.

It was supposed to be a flying unicorn in a snowstorm. I thought it was dumb. My secret pal didn't even know how to spell my name.

On Wednesday, I got a drawing of a snowman and one sentence:

It was a one-eyed snowman.

Ho, ho, ho, I thought. It was so funny, I forgot to laugh.

Thursday, Song Lee found a clay salamander on her desk. There was a story next to it. The story was three pages long.

I could tell Song Lee liked the salamander because she named it Lin Woo

and made a collar of flowers for it.

When Harry came back from the lavatory, he had another note and surprise on his desk. It was a pencil holder made out of a ball of aluminum foil. Three holes were jabbed in it for pencils.

Harry read his note:

Dear Harry

I Know you like to rite storys so here is something to hold your pencils. And when you are board you can take the pencils out and play catch with it.

Your Pal ?

"See?" Harry said. "My secret pal knows how to be a friend. Are you going to change your mind and tell me who your secret pal is?"

I shook my head.

"Then I'm not even going to talk to you anymore."

Harry was acting *so* horrible I didn't even care if he was my best friend anymore.

When I came back from the pencil sharpener, I found a folded piece of paper on my desk. Probably another dumb letter from Frosty. I opened it.

The note had two sentences this time.

Sorry pal
I just have one crayon
and it's red.
Frosty

Friday morning everyone was excited about finding out who his secret pal was. Except me.

Miss Mackle passed out the homework letters. "Now you will find out who your secret pal is!

Song Lee turned as red as a salamander when she found out it was Harry. I think she knew who it was all along though. She turned red because Harry drew a heart on his letter.

I read mine. It said:

Dear DuG
You got Luckey.
You got me for a secret
Pal
From
Sidney

I thought it was from someone like Sidney.

Harry finally got around to opening his letter. It was folded five times about the size of a lemon.

Harry read it outloud:

Dear Harry,

We were best friends before
we became secret pals. Now
we dont even talk. Or play
I still dont feel Like tellin
g you who I am ?

Harry looked at me, "YOU! I should have guessed! You didn't want to spoil the surprise."

I didn't say anything. I just looked

ahead at the classroom calendar for December.

I could see from the corner of my eye that Harry was writing something. Then drawing something. Then he pushed it under my elbow.

I acted like it wasn't there. I wanted to count how many days were in December. There were thirty-one.

Slowly, I moved the paper in front of me and I read it.

DEEr Doug
I Am Sore. WILL you forgiv mE?
Yur budE forever
HArry

P.S. Here is
A Pickchur of A TArAnCHyuLa
And A SLug →

I turned and looked at Harry.

He was smiling so hard I could see his two silver fillings in the back.

Sometimes when Harry is really horrible, he apologizes.

And sometimes, I forgive him.

The Deadly Skit

One day after lunch, the principal, Mr. Cardini came into the classroom. He was not happy. He was holding something in his fingers that was long and white. "*This* was found under a cafeteria table." Everyone leaned forward to see what it was.

"It's a cigarette," he said.

We all groaned.

"Although it was not lit, someone in South School thinks cigarettes are okay to have around. Cigarettes are *not* okay. They are bad for your health. Smoking can kill you. Now, I'm asking each classroom to do some kind of activity that will promote a NO SMOKING Campaign at South School."

As we nodded our heads, Miss Mackle looked at Mr. Cardini. "Room 2B will do something special about it," she said.

Mr. Cardini waved to us and then he left the classroom.

"Let's make posters!" Sidney blurted out.

I raised my hand. "Yes, Doug," Miss Mackle replied.

"I'm tired of doing posters. We did fire prevention posters just last week."

"That's true," Ida said. "No one even got an honorable mention in our room."

"Would you like to do skits?" Miss Mackle suggested.

"Yeah!" we all shouted.

"Well then," Miss Mackle continued, "I will put you in groups of six. You can get together and plan something. Of course the main idea is . . . smoking is bad for you."

Harry and I looked at each other and

crossed our fingers. We wanted to be on the same committee.

Miss Mackle got her roll book. "Okay, in this corner, we can have these people practice—Doug, Sidney, Ida, Mary, Song Lee, and . . ."

Harry was kneeling on the floor begging to be chosen.

". . . and, okay, Harry."

Harry and I jumped in the air!

"Together!" we said in a thumb grip.

As we walked over to the corner,

Mary spoke first. "Everyone sit Indian style in a circle."

Harry rolled his eyeballs, but he did what Mary said. I did too. "Now," she said. "I think we should sing something about not smoking. I can even play the song on the piano."

We looked over at Miss Mackle's piano. It had a lot of stuff on it.

"I don't like to sing," Sidney complained.

"I do. My favorite song is 'Silent Night,' " Ida replied. "We're singing it in the church choir."

"I can play 'Silent Night' on the piano," Mary said.

"I don't like to sing," Sidney repeated.

"I like 'Silent Night,' too," Song Lee said. "It is only song I know English word to."

I shook my head. "Listen you guys. This is NOT a Christmas program. It's supposed to be about not smoking."

"Doug's right," Sidney agreed. "Besides, I don't want to sing. I just want to be king."

"King?" I replied. "Who said there was a king in our skit?"

Harry raised his eyebrows and spoke for the first time. Hmmmm, kings do smoke I suppose." And then he said, "hmmmm," again.

I could tell Harry's wheels were turning. "I think I can put all of this together," he said.

"You can?" Mary replied.

"Yes," Harry said. "Our skit is about death."

"DEATH?" we asked.

"Smoking kills," Harry said. "You heard the principal."

Ida spoke up, "I'm not going to be the one who dies—that's for sure!"

"Me either," Mary said. "That's a horrible part."

Harry grinned. "We need three people to die. I'm one."

"I'll be the other," I said. "I'm not afraid to pretend that I'm dead."

"Not me," Sidney said. "No way. Playing dead is creepy."

Song Lee spoke softly, "It is true. Cigarette make you not have long life. I die for skit." And then she added, "Do I have to say anything before I die?"

"You don't have to. You just have to stand up with Doug and me and look like a king."

"A KING! I WANT TO BE A KING!" Sidney shouted.

Miss Mackle came over to us. "How are we doing? Is there a problem?"

Sidney answered right away. "Harry is bossing everyone around."

"Is that true?" the teacher asked us.

Song Lee shook her head. "We talk. Harry listen. Now Harry has good idea for skit."

Miss Mackle smiled and moved on to the next group.

"Look Sidney," Harry said. "If you want to be a king you have to be willing to die. The king in this skit dies."

Sidney looked like he was going to cry. "Can the king just be wounded? I could play a wounded king."

"The king dies, Sidney," Harry replied.

"Then I won't be one," Sidney said.

"Can I play the piano?" Mary said with her hands folded.

"Yes. And we will need two angels," Harry added.

Ida jumped up and down. "Good! I get to be an angel."

Sidney shook his head. "I'm not going to be any angel. Girls are angels. Not boys."

Mary disagreed. "There are boy angels and girl angels. Heaven is a fair place."

Harry continued, "We'll need three blankets and three crowns for the kings and halos and sheets for the angels."

"Some choice," Sidney complained. "A dead king or a dumb angel."

Mary put her hands on her hips. "Angels are not dumb. They are perfect beans."

"Kidney or lima beings?" Sidney asked. And then he cackled and giggled.

"Have you made your choice?" Harry

asked Sidney when he was through cackling.

"Yeah, I'll be a kidney bean."

Nobody said anything. Just Sidney. He laughed by himself.

We brought the props and costumes in the next day. Song Lee brought in gold garland for the halos, and aluminum foil and buttons and sequins for the crowns.

"My mother sew," Song Lee said. "She has many thing."

We worked hard on the props the next day. We practiced the singing part of our skit at recess because we wanted it to be a surprise.

Friday afternoon, we had a little theater. Miss Mackle called on the four groups to perform. When it was our turn, Harry introduced us.

"And now—" he said. "We are happy

to present 'The Deadly Skit.' "

Miss Mackle backed up against the blackboard. A piece of chalk fell and shattered into tiny pieces.

Harry, Song Lee, and I stood in front of the class. We had blankets around us and crowns on our heads. They sparkled with sequins.

Mary started to play on the piano.

We began to sing: "We three kings of Orientar, tried to smoke a smelly cigar. . . ."

Then we started puffing on a Tootsie Roll. (Harry had brought those in.) Song Lee fell to the ground coughing and choking and rolling over until she died.

Harry and I continued singing. Mary continued playing. "We two kings of Orientar, tried to smoke a smelly cigar. . . ."

Then I fell down to the ground coughing and choking and rolling over until I died.

Harry was the only king left. "I the king of Orientar, tried to smoke a smelly cigar. . . ."

When Harry fell down to the ground coughing and choking and rolling over, the two angels entered.

They had white sheets draped around them with garland halos pinned in their hair. Sidney didn't look very happy with bobby pins in his hair.

After Harry died, Ida and Sidney sang, "Silent Night, Holy Night. All is calm. All is bright."

Miss Mackle began clapping her

hands. "They certainly got the message across that smoking shortens your life! Bravo!"

Everyone in the class joined her.

Mary took a special bow from the piano.

Thanks to Harry, our skit about something horrible was the best one in the class.

Invasion of the Cobwebs

One morning Harry came into Room 2B and put his head down on his desk.

"You sick?" I asked.

"Yeah, Doug. I'm sick of South School. Nothing ever happens around here. The place is getting boring."

Just as Harry closed his eyes, Miss Mackle walked in. She pulled up her reading chair and sat in front of the class. "I'm going to begin our day by finishing our book, *Charlotte's Web.*"

Everyone cheered. The best part of the day is when Miss Mackle reads to us. She chooses good books.

When Miss Mackle came to the part where Charlotte was dying, she started to get tears in her eyes. "I have to stop for a moment, class," she said.

I looked over at Song Lee. She had a flowered hanky out. When I looked over at Harry, I was shocked. One big fat tear rolled out of his eyeball and down his cheek.

Suddenly Harry blurted out, "Why does Charlotte have to die?"

Miss Mackle put her book down on her lap. "We all do sometime. Dying is a part of life. A spider just doesn't live very long."

2B

"Now Wilbur will be all alone," Ida whimpered.

"The story is not over," Miss Mackle replied as she picked up the book. "Wilbur is going to have some new friends. You'll see."

Everyone listened as Miss Mackle finished the book. When she read the last page, everyone just stared into space smiling.

Miss Mackle stood up and placed the book on her desk. As she looked out the window at the snow flurries, she thought aloud, "After you read a great story like *Charlotte's Web,* you don't feel like just doing the next thing. . . ."

And then she looked down at her lesson plans. ". . . reviewing plurals and action words," she mumbled.

I raised my hand.

"Yes, Doug?"

"Why don't we celebrate *Charlotte's Web?*" I said.

Miss Mackle looked up from her lesson plans. "Why don't we! Let's take the entire morning doing an activity that shows our love for Charlotte!"

"What can we do?" Sidney asked.

Just then Harry stood up and acted like he had the biggest idea in the whole world. "I got it! Let's plan an invasion of South School!"

Oh boy, I thought. Harry and his horrible ideas.

Miss Mackle put her hands on her hips. "WHAT does an invasion have to do with celebrating *Charlotte's Web*?"

"Everything!" Harry replied as he waved his hands in the air. "We each make a cobweb and put it somewhere around the school. We could launch an invasion of the cobwebs!"

Miss Mackle thought about it. "Hmmmm. . . . An invasion of cobwebs. I LOVE IT!"

Harry beamed.

"Let's get busy," she said, "and let South School know how much we loved the book!"

We cheered and clapped as Miss Mackle passed out black construction paper, scissors, and white chalk.

We spent a lot of time making the cobwebs. Some people put Charlotte or her grandchildren in the web. Song Lee remembered the cobwebs in the story and wrote what Charlotte did, *HUMBLE*. Mary and Ida copied Song Lee. They made webs with *RADIANT* and *TERRIFIC* in the middle.

Harry put something different in the middle of his web. He made a spider rolling up a fly and sucking its blood.

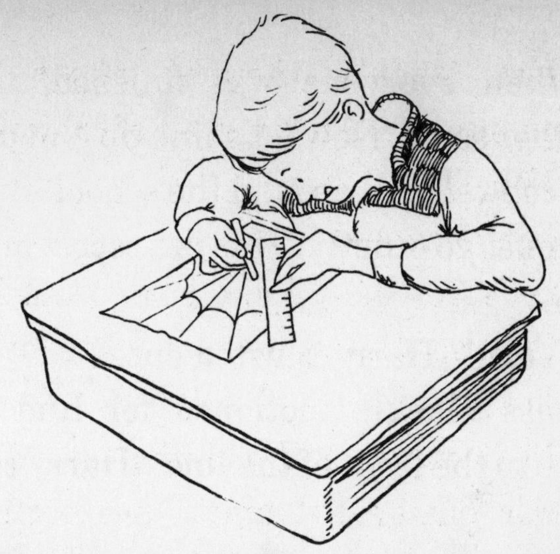

"This one is for the principal's office," he grinned.

Sidney cackled.

I used a ruler when I made my web. Then I made Charlotte's egg sac—her magnum opus hanging down from the web.

Miss Mackle walked up and down the aisles. You could tell she was pleased. She said something nice about each one. Even Harry's.

"Spiders have to eat too," she said.

When everyone was finished, the teacher said, "Now let's line up and put our cobwebs all around the school. But, we must go quietly. This is a secret mission!"

"Yeah!" Harry blurted out.

Miss Mackle motioned for him to come to the front of the line. "Harry can

be our line leader since this invasion was his idea."

Harry walked proudly to the front of the line. Then he gave me back cuts.

"Be thinking of good places to tape your webs," Miss Mackle said. "Think about where Charlotte might like to spin hers."

Very quietly we walked down the hall.

"After you find a place to put your web," Miss Mackle whispered, "go to the end of the line."

When Ida taped her cobweb in the doorway of the secretary's office, the secretary, Mrs. Foxworth, looked up and jerked back. Her pencil fell off her ear and into her coffee cup.

"How nice!" she said reading the cob-web. But she wasn't smiling. Every-

one could tell she didn't like spiders.

Mary put her cobweb down by the girls lavatory. Two little kindergartners who were washing their hands asked, "Why did you put that there?"

"To celebrate a great story about a spider."

"You mean the spider that sat next to Miss Muffet?"

"Good guess, but that's not the right spider," Mary replied. "Keep guessing!"

Sidney put his cobweb in the computer room. The computer teacher, Mr. Landers, asked, "Are you saying that my room is dusty by putting that spider in it?"

Sidney cackled, "Nope! Guess again. It's an important reason!

Mr. Landers tried to think harder.

I put my magnum opus on the back of the librarian's chair. Mrs. Michaelsen didn't even see me do it. She was reading.

Song Lee put her cobweb with *HUMBLE* on it hanging from the school stairwell.

Miss Mackle helped some children who wanted their webs next to EXIT signs and over the tops of doors.

When we got to the principal's office, Harry tiptoed inside. Mr. Cardini was on the phone. He had his back to Harry. Very quietly, Harry taped his cobweb to the principal's closet door.

When all twenty-four cobwebs were put somewhere in South School, we hurried back to class.

As soon as everyone was in their seats, Miss Mackle waved her hands in the air. "We did it! What fun!"

Everyone clapped their hands.

Just then Mr. Cardini showed up at

the door. Everyone stopped cheering. He was holding Harry's cobweb in his hand. "What is the meaning of this?" he said, pointing to the bloody spider.

Miss Mackle's voice was shaking, "We . . . we . . ."

Harry stood up and finished her sentence, "It's an invasion of cobwebs to celebrate *Charlotte's Web*. We love that book."

"And now," Mr. Cardini said in a loud, booming voice, "we have spider webs ALL OVER SOUTH SCHOOL!"

Everyone slowly nodded their head.

Miss Mackle did too.

"Even one on my closet door!" he added waving it in the air.

And then Mr. Cardini started to smile, "I love it! It's a wonderful idea! Now I just have to put this cobweb back where it belongs. On my door!"

When he left the room, Miss Mackle looked at us and laughed.

We did too.

Sometimes Harry's horrible ideas make South School an exciting place.

Demonstrations

Miss Mackle gave Room 2B a homework assignment for Friday. "I want you to demonstrate to the class how to do something," she said.

Mary raised her hand, "Can I show how I braid my hair each morning?"

"That would be a good demonstration," Miss Mackle said.

I looked over at Harry. He was thinking already. At lunch when he was twirling the spaghetti around his fork he said, "I could bring my microscope to class and show how to make a slide."

"What would you look at on the slide?" I asked chomping into some garlic bread.

"Easy," Harry replied. "I'd prick my finger and put a drop of blood on the slide."

"Eeyew! Blood!" Ida said as she joined us at the lunch table.

"Blood is beautiful under the microscope," Harry replied.

"Blood is horrible," Mary said sitting down next to Ida and Song Lee.

"But," I said, "it would take too long for the class to take turns to look at the slide."

"Probably," Harry agreed.

"I am going to demonstrate how to weave on a loom," Ida said. "I can make pot holders and other things. Mostly, pot holders though. I have eleven at home."

"What are you doing Song Lee?" Harry asked.

"I don't like to speak in front of class," she said.

"How long have you been in America?" Harry asked.

"I come to America one year ago."

"You speak very well," Harry replied. "Want to be my assistant?"

Song Lee beamed. "I help you Harry. What is your demonstration?"

Harry grinned, "How to make green slime."

"Aaauuugh!" Ida and Mary replied.

"I help make green slime," Song Lee said.

Friday morning, everyone came to school with boxes and bags of stuff. Miss Mackle moved a long table in front of the class so we would have a platform to work on. She also invited the librarian, Mrs. Michaelsen, and the principal, Mr. Cardini.

They sat in the back of the room on small chairs.

Mary went first. She brought her doll and demonstrated how to braid hair.

Ida went second. She showed how to make a pot holder on her loom. When she finished she gave it to Miss Mackle.

"I don't get one?" Mr. Cardini complained from the back of the room.

Everyone laughed.

"I'll bring you one from home," Ida said.

When it was Sidney's turn, everyone waited for him to unpack his big sack.

"Today, I am going to demonstrate how to make a canary out of tinker toys."

Harry made a face.

I shook my head.

Everyone watched as Sidney put round pieces into sticks, and then made it stand alone on the table.

"That's a canary!" He said.

Everyone clapped except Harry and me.

My turn was next. I stood up with my bag of stuff and walked to the platform.

"I need an assistant," I said.

Everyone raised his hand except Song Lee. She was waiting to be Harry's assistant.

"Me! Me! Me!" Sidney shouted out.

"I'd like to volunteer!" a voice said from the back of the room.

Everyone turned. It was the principal!

"YES!!" everyone called out. "The principal!"

I was beginning to get nervous. I wasn't planning on working with . . . the principal!

"I guess I'm elected," Mr. Cardini said.

Everyone watched Mr. Cardini

come to the front of the room.

"Are you sure you want to do this?" I whispered to the principal.

"This is the best part about my job," he whispered back to me. "I get to have a little fun!"

I took a deep breath, and pointed to the teacher's big reading chair. "Please be seated, sir," I said.

The principal sat down and faced the class.

I took a plastic cape out of my bag and carefully put it around the principal. Then I tied it behind his neck.

"Today," I said, "I am going to demonstrate how to . . ."

All the kids were half off their seats watching and listening.

". . . how to spike your hair."

"OOOOHH!" the class shouted.

Miss Mackle needed a chair. She

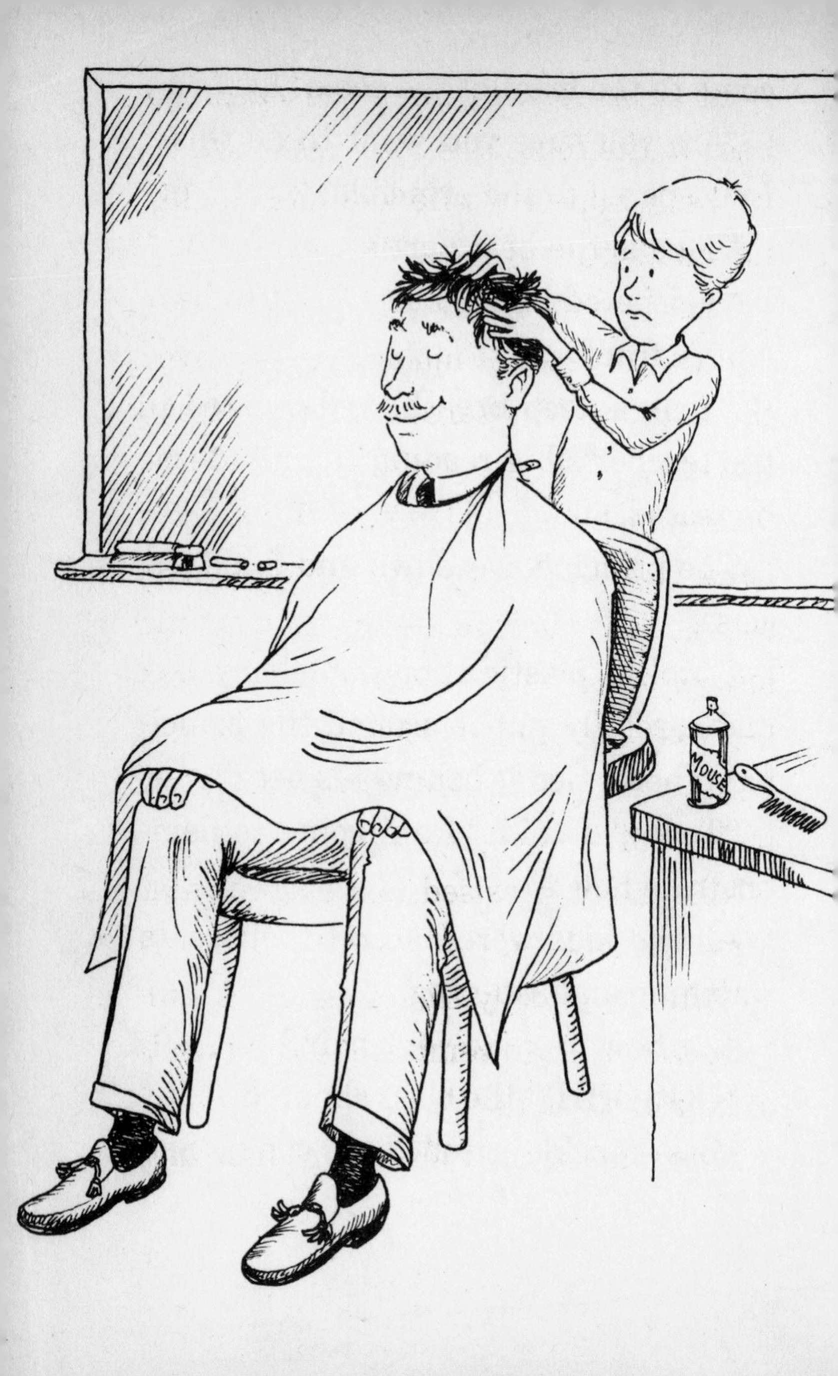
MOUSE

went to sit next to the librarian in the back of the room.

"Let's hope my wife will like it," Mr. Cardini said.

The class laughed.

I took my can of mousse and sprayed the foam on Mr. Cardini's hair. He had lots of it.

Slowly I rubbed the stuff into his head. It was a funny feeling to be massaging the principal's head. But he had lots of good hair to work with. I was beginning to enjoy myself.

"Ahhhh . . ." Mr. Cardini said. "That feels good."

Miss Mackle raised her eyebrows at Mrs. Michaelsen.

"After you apply the mousse," I said, "you take a clean comb and comb hunks of hair out like this."

Everytime I took a hunk of hair and

combed it out, the class laughed.

Miss Mackle was sinking in her chair.

When I took the last hunk of hair and combed it out, I said, "There! Mr. Cardini has spiked hair."

Everyone applauded.

I handed the principal a mirror and he looked at himself.

"*Bravisimo!*" he said. "I think my wife just might take me out to dinner tonight!"

The class laughed.

This time Miss Mackle and Mrs. Michaelsen did too.

Harry and Song Lee were last.

"Today," Harry said, "my assistant Song Lee and I are going to make green slime for you."

Everyone groaned and then oohed.

"It's a scientist's dream!" Harry

grinned. "May I have a bowl please?"

Song Lee handed Harry a bowl.

"Cornstarch," Harry said.

Song Lee handed Harry a box of cornstarch.

"Measuring cup."

Song Lee handed Harry a measuring cup.

Everyone in the audience turned their head from side to side as they watched Song Lee pass things to Harry.

"First," Harry said, "you measure one cup of cornstarch into a bowl."

"Then you measure half a cup of water and pour it into the bowl. Water please."

Song Lee handed Harry a pitcher of water.

Harry measured it and then poured it into the bowl.

"Stir, and then add . . ." Harry held

out his hand like he wanted a scalpel or some tool.

Song Lee handed Harry a small bottle of food coloring.

"Squeeze three drops of green into the bowl. Stir and there you have it—GREEN SLIME!"

The class watched Harry pour the slime out of the bowl onto a sheet of wax paper. It poured like a liquid but when Harry put a spoon in it, it cracked in half.

"It's magic!" Sidney blurted out.

Everyone clapped.

Mrs. Michaelsen asked what Harry was going to do with the green slime now that his demonstration was over.

"Throw it out. My mom said she didn't want any more slime at our house."

"May I have it then? I'd like to show it to my husband. He's interested in science."

Harry wrapped the green slime up in the waxed paper and handed it to the librarian.

"Thank you boys and girls for a great afternoon," Mrs. Michaelsen said as she walked out the door with Mr. Cardini.

"Me too," the principal said. And he went back to his office with his spiked hairdo.

Mrs. Foxworth, who was typing a letter, looked up and jerked back. The pencil that was on her ear went flying across her desk, hit the wall, and landed in the garbage can.

Bull's-eye!

Harry and I are glad we're at South School. Our teacher, principal, and librarian aren't afraid of anything horrible.

Only our school secretary is.